To Cher—
Friend, Chef, and Trier of New Things

Text and illustrations copyright © 2015 by Mo Willems

All rights reserved. Published by Hyperion Books for Children, an imprint of Disney Book Group. No part of this book may be reproduced or transmitted in any form or by any means, electronic or mechanical, including photocopying, recording, or by any information storage and retrieval system, without written permission from the publisher. For information address Hyperion Books for Children, 125 West End Avenue, New York, New York 10023.

Library of Congress Cataloging-in-Publication Data

Willems, Mo, author, illustrator.
 I really like slop! / by Mo Willems.—First edition.
     pages cm.—(An Elephant & Piggie book)
 Summary: "Piggie really likes slop. She likes it so much, she wants Gerald to try some! But can Gerald find the courage to do it? Or will the smell alone be too much to handle?"—Provided by publisher.
 ISBN 978-1-4847-2262-6
[1. Food habits—Fiction. 2. Friendship—Fiction. 3. Elephants—Fiction. 4. Pigs—Fiction.] I. Title.
 PZ7.W65535Iap 2015
 [E]—dc23   2014041976

Visit www.hyperionbooksforchildren.com and www.pigeonpresents.com

Printed in the United States of America
Reinforced binding

First Edition, November 2015
10 9 8 7 6 5 4 3 2 1
F322-8368-8-15227

Hyperion Books for Children / *New York*

AN IMPRINT OF DISNEY BOOK GROUP

An ELEPHANT & PIGGIE Book

5

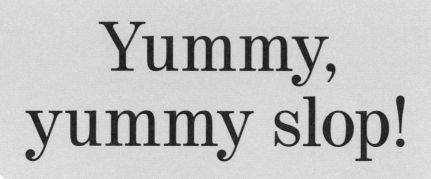

POP!

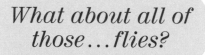

25

WALK WALK WALK WALK

Piggie.

I will

GULP!

try your slop.

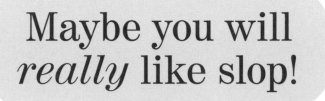

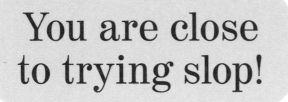

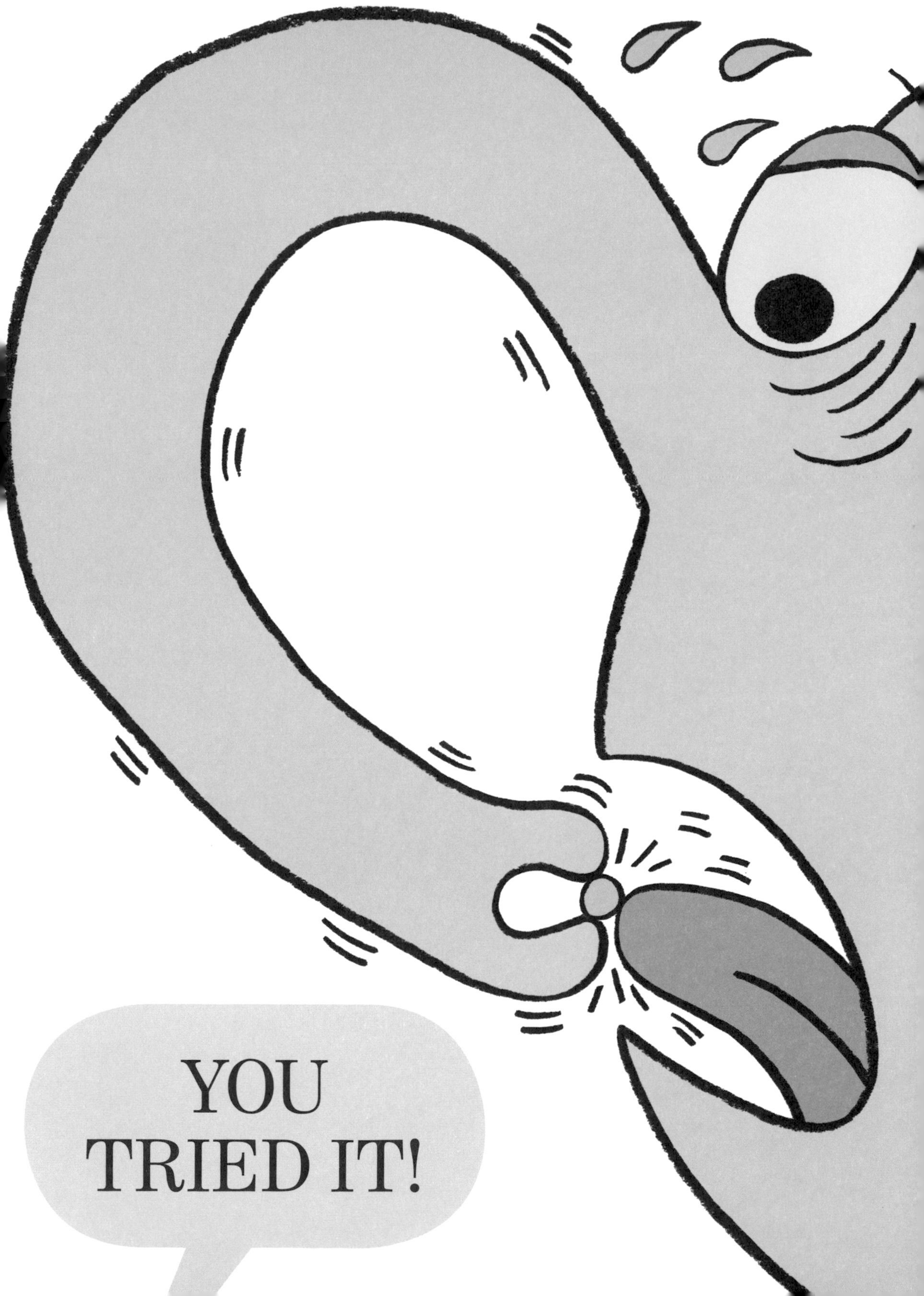
YOU TRIED IT!

Elephant and Piggie have more funny adventures in:

Today I Will Fly!

My Friend Is Sad

I Am Invited to a Party!

There Is a Bird on Your Head!
(Theodor Seuss Geisel Medal)

I Love My New Toy!

I Will Surprise My Friend!

Are You Ready to Play Outside?
(Theodor Seuss Geisel Medal)

Watch Me Throw the Ball!

Elephants Cannot Dance!

Pigs Make Me Sneeze!

I Am Going!

Can I Play Too?

We Are in a Book!
(Theodor Seuss Geisel Honor)

I Broke My Trunk!
(Theodor Seuss Geisel Honor)

Should I Share My Ice Cream?

Happy Pig Day!

Listen to My Trumpet!

Let's Go for a Drive!
(Theodor Seuss Geisel Honor)

A Big Guy Took My Ball!
(Theodor Seuss Geisel Honor)

I'm a Frog!

My New Friend Is So Fun!

Waiting Is Not Easy!
(Theodor Seuss Geisel Honor)

I Will Take a Nap!